Buffalo Home

by Linda Baxter

COVER-TO-COVER BOOKS

Perfection Learning®

Cover and Inside
Illustration: Dan Hatala

For Kathy and Ann

About the Author

Linda Baxter was born in Cheyenne, Wyoming, and traveled with her military family, finally settling in Tempe, Arizona. She graduated with a degree in elementary education from Arizona State University. Ms. Baxter taught elementary grades in Phoenix, Arizona, and Catshill, Bromsgrove, England.

She lives with her husband, Dave, and three children in Monte Sereno, California.

Perfection Learning® Corporation

1000 North Second Avenue, P.O. Box 500

Logan, Iowa 51546-0500.

Phone: 1-800-831-4190

Fax: 1-800-543-2745

perfectionlearning.com

Paperback ISBN 0-7891-5679-2

Cover Craft® ISBN 0-7569-0670-9

Contents

1

Beginning

The roar of the plane's small engines numbed Miguel's ears. He peered out the small window of the 12-passenger aircraft and studied the barren brown hills below. He traced an almost dry riverbed as it snaked through a distant valley.

Great, thought Miguel in disgust. This is the middle of nowhere. I'm going to be out of here in no time, he decided. I'm not going to be stuck on any stupid reservation.

The plane suddenly dipped, leaving Miguel's stomach a few thousand feet above. He spotted the lonely airport. It wasn't crammed in the middle of a city like the one he had left behind in Phoenix. This airport had jackrabbits for neighbors.

The sun hung low in the sky. It had been a long day. Miguel sat back and held on to his stomach. He didn't have butterflies just because of the turbulence. His stomach twisted at the thought of what was to come. He brushed his long dark hair away from his face. Stubbornly, he ordered his dark eyes not to tear.

The plane landed with wheels screeching. It headed for the small terminal. Miguel walked across the runway. Head up, shoulders back, Miguel tried to make his small frame bigger. He mounted the stairs to the waiting room.

The other passengers soon found their greeters. Miguel hung back.

Then the shadow of a huge man covered him.

"Miguel," said the man. It was not a question.

"Miguel," the big man repeated. "My name is David Small Bear. I have come for you."

Miguel looked up. Don't look scared, he thought. Then he nodded quickly. The man turned and moved away through the airport crowd. Miguel could only follow.

The squeaks and rattles of the old Bronco lulled Miguel. He'd been up since before dawn. Now dusk closed in on the narrow two-lane road. Shadows crept across the prairie. The big man had said nothing since they began their journey.

Miguel must have fallen asleep. In a dream, he felt someone shaking his shoulder.

"Miguel, Miguel," his foster mother called mildly. "It's time to get up and start your big trip."

Miguel groaned.

"Come on now. We can't be late for the plane," she said cheerfully.

Miguel wanted to hide under the warm covers. The foster home wasn't fancy, but at least he knew what to do there. He didn't want to go live in South Dakota. He didn't want a new family.

Miguel and his foster mother drove through the early dawn. The streets were empty. He waved good-bye . . .

A bump slammed him against the truck door. Miguel awoke. He tried frantically to remember where he was.

Silently, Miguel studied the big man's face from under the hair hanging over his eyes. There is nothing small about David Small Bear, thought Miguel. David's head almost touched the top of the Bronco. His shoulders filled the seat. Black hair, straight and thick, was pulled back from his deeply tanned face. A braid hung down his back.

"You look like an Indian," said Miguel bluntly. He didn't care. He wasn't sticking around here.

David's face relaxed into a smile. "Suppose I do," he agreed.

What am I doing here? wondered Miguel. How will I get away? There was so much "nothing" here. How do you get away from all this nothing?

Miguel studied the government sign that announced the Pine Ridge Indian Reservation. Without thinking, Miguel let out a sigh.

"The reservation is not a prison, Miguel. Not now anyway. Once, long ago, it was a prison for the Lakota. But now there are good things here—good people," said the big man.

Miguel didn't believe him. Why did you have to die, Mama? he cried silently inside.

2

Tatanka (Buffalo)

It was dark when the Bronco bumped up the rutted drive to the little shack that David called home. Home, Miguel thought in despair. It was so small! And it was built of thin pine logs that formed the walls on the inside too.

The man showed Miguel his room, a loft above the kitchen. The attic had only one small window. The bed was soft with a thick, warm blanket. It was even red— his favorite color. Exhausted, Miguel lay down to rest.

He stared out the window into the black night. He remembered the tubes, the whirring machines, and the hospital waiting room. Most of all, he recalled his mother's ghostly face.

"You have to be brave, Miguel," his mom had said.

"I'm trying," he whispered now.

Miguel was awake at sunrise. He climbed down the ladder. The cabin was silent. The cracked linoleum felt cold on his bare feet.

It wasn't time to leave yet—not today. He just wanted to take a look around. Miguel didn't know what the big man expected, but he sure wasn't going to cooperate.

Miguel snatched an apple from the small counter that served as a kitchen. Quietly, he unlocked the door.

Other than a squeak of the hinge as the door shut, he was outside without a sound. Miguel gasped at the morning view.

The house was nestled in a hollow near the top of a high hill. The door of the cabin faced east. As Miguel looked out, the sun greeted him with unexpected warmth. Miles of grass stretched gold and green in front of him. A river wound its way along the base of the valley. The valley was sprinkled with willows and cottonwoods. The leaves were golden and shimmering.

Looking out over the valley below, he could see one other small house in the distance. The sun had just edged over the top of the opposite hill. In the new light, Miguel studied the strange rock formations. They looked like white castle walls.

Miguel was used to barren hills. Arizona had mountains of stark red rock. They were dotted with cacti that looked like creatures from another planet. He was also used to Phoenix—the busy streets, the packed apartment buildings, the crowds of people. Did anyone live in South Dakota?

"The Lakota always faced their tipis with the door to the east. That way the brave can face the morning and give thanks to the Great Mystery," said David.

Miguel eyed the big man suspiciously. He hadn't heard him approach.

David stretched and asked Miguel, "Hungry?"

Miguel shrugged, but his face betrayed him.

"Hmm. Thought so. You conked out on me last night. Let's go see if we can find something to eat," said David. He started across the narrow yard.

"What are we going to eat?" sneered Miguel. "Grass?"

"Come find out," called David over his shoulder. He kept walking.

Miguel followed David down the hill. Around a small bend stood an old barn and a small shed. Long fences captured chunks of prairie.

David headed for the shed. He unlatched the rope hook. The hinges squealed. Inside, a noisy crowd greeted him.

"Morning, ladies," called David cheerfully.

Miguel followed curiously. He peeked into the dim interior. Shelves lined both sides. They were stuffed with hay.

"Good job, Mathilda and Sophie," congratulated David.

"Who are you talking to?" asked Miguel.

"My chickens," explained David. "Here's breakfast." He held up two grubby-looking eggs.

Yuck, thought Miguel.

"Madeline is off her nest. You can get her egg," David instructed. He gently pushed another chicken aside and gathered a third egg.

Miguel inched forward.

David pointed to the nest. "Go on," he encouraged. "Sometimes Madeline will fight you tooth and nail for her egg. I guess she knew we had a beginner on our hands."

Miguel reached into the nest and grasped the still-warm egg.

"Come on," said David. He stepped back into the sunshine. "Do you know how to cook?" he asked.

Miguel didn't reply. He just trailed behind David in silence, eyes down.

Back in the cabin, David fixed breakfast. On a small butane stove, the big man scrambled their eggs.

The eggs looked different from store eggs. They had bright orange yolks. But they tasted delicious. Miguel cleaned his plate with a crust of bread.

"I'll show you how to use the stove in a day or two. For now, I'll cook and you can wash. Deal?" David asked.

Miguel shrugged and studied him secretly. "Sometimes I cooked for my mom," he finally admitted.

David nodded as he got up from the table. While Miguel washed the dishes, David disappeared for a few minutes. He returned wearing boots and a large cowboy hat.

"Ready?" he asked, standing by the door.

Miguel followed him down the road to the fenced pasture. A couple of horses greeted them with whinnies.

They continued on to a pasture near the bottom of the hill. Miguel peered through the rails. He caught movement behind a few scrubby trees.

David whistled loudly. The bushes rustled. A strange humphing sound replied. More rustling followed. Another whistle brought out a huge, dark beast with horns and fierce eyes.

Cool, thought Miguel.

"See that small plant there with the thick white leaves?" asked David. He pointed near Miguel's feet. "Break off a piece of that. It's white sage. Bossy is a pushover for it. She's eaten every nibble in her pasture."

When Miguel tugged at the plant, a strong spicy fragrance caught his nose. He sniffed at the plant.

"Buffalo love sage," David explained. "Now wave it at Bossy."

"I've never seen a buffalo before," said Miguel. He held out the white leaves. "Except at the zoo in Phoenix," he added.

"This is where they come from. This is where they belong," answered David.

Miguel waved the white leaves. The buffalo began to trot across the pasture. It gathered speed, galloping and humphing again.

"Whoa!" shouted Miguel, pulling back. A buffalo was very big up close.

"She won't hurt you," David assured Miguel. "Go on. She'll be your friend for life."

The buffalo wedged her huge head through the fence. Her hot breath blew in Miguel's face. Slowly, he handed her the sage. She carefully chomped it, pulling back when she saw there was no more. Her big brown eyes studied him thoughtfully.

"Cool," said Miguel. "Where did you get her?"

The big man scratched between the huge animal's horns. "Good girl. How's my baby?" he crooned.

"She's an orphan," he explained to Miguel. "Raised her myself. We went to the roundup a few years back—my dad and I. Somehow she had been separated from her mother. I took her home and bottle-fed her. She'll have her calf in the spring."

Miguel studied the huge head. He looked into the deep, trusting eyes. A thick bushy mane covered the front half of the buffalo. A long tail swished at her shiny haunches.

"She's not like most buffalo," warned David. "She's really more of a pet. Most buffalo are wild or pretty close to it. You shouldn't get too near," he explained.

"There are more?" asked Miguel.

"I have a hundred head so far. I've only been ranching for two years. Before I'm done, I'll grow the herd to a thousand," said David with pride.

"That's a lot," said Miguel.

"There used to be millions." The man shook his head sadly. "But that was long ago."

3

Tiyospaye (Family)

Miguel and David were sitting at the back of the house watching the sun set.

"Tomorrow, you'll start at Red Cloud School," David said.

Miguel couldn't help the sigh that escaped.

"You don't like school?" asked David.

"I just hate starting at a new one," said Miguel. He had lost count of the schools he had attended.

Then he admitted, "I always get teased. I'm not as tall as most of the kids in the sixth grade."

"It's a good school," David assured him. "I went there. Even my father went there back when it was a boarding school."

"Can I give Bossy some more sage when I get home?" asked Miguel.

David nodded. "You'll grow, Miguel."

The Bronco bumped down the rutted trail and back onto the narrow highway.

"It's barely light," complained Miguel.

"It's a long way," explained David.

They barreled down the two-lane road. They stopped only once for two deer that were crossing. Then they followed a long yellow school bus the rest of the way. A small boy made faces out the back window of the bus. David made a face back. Miguel tried not to smile.

"Many kids travel a lot farther than you to go to school on the reservation," David pointed out. "Some even come from 90 miles away. You only have to go about 20."

"Piece of cake," mumbled Miguel. The butterflies were back.

Together they entered the office of a huge, old brick building. Miguel took off for the classroom by himself.

"Take bus nine home," David reminded. "I'll meet you at the bottom of our hill."

The class was silent as Miguel entered the room. Twenty-five pairs of eyes watched him shuffle to a chair in the back. He sat, head down, hiding behind his hair.

Class continued with history and math lessons. Miguel knew the answers to the history questions and the math problems, but he didn't raise his hand.

"Time for your Lakota lesson," his teacher announced. The class moved together down the hall. Miguel dragged his feet.

The language teacher spoke to the class in Lakota. Miguel knew some Spanish from his school in Phoenix, and he was good at it. He had even taught a little to his mom. But this wasn't Spanish.

"Miguel? I just said 'please sit down,' " said the teacher. Miguel blushed. One girl giggled, but the teacher's quick look squelched that.

"My name is Miss LaPierre. Have you had any Lakota lessons before? Do you speak it at home?" asked the pretty teacher. She had soft brown eyes. They were large like the eyes of the fawn he had seen on the highway. Her hair hung long down her back.

Miguel shook his head. The butterflies were back.

"Never mind. You are home now, Miguel. You are with your family. We will all help you learn your language," she spoke softly.

Miguel wished she were right, but he knew that he was all alone. He sat hunched in his chair.

The rest of the day passed slowly for Miguel. He was relieved when school was finally dismissed.

Miguel sat at the back of the bus. No one bothered him. The high school boys were talking about the football game. Two little girls were playing with dolls.

David was waiting for him at the bottom of their hill. Miguel shuffled off the bus. Then he ran ahead to find some sage.

Miguel wasn't so afraid this time when Bossy stuck her huge head through the fence. He rubbed her big wet nose as she chewed the spicy sage. "Humph," she sighed happily.

"How was the first day?" asked David.

Miguel shrugged.

They headed up the hill. Miguel slung his backpack over his shoulder. He hurried along, trying to keep up with the big man's stride.

"What is Lakota?" Miguel asked after a while.

"*We* are the Lakota," David explained. "We are part

of a great nation. Some call it the Sioux Nation."

Miguel was still confused.

"Didn't your mother teach you about who you are?" asked David.

"She said we were part Indian, but that was all. I never had a father. My mom . . ." Miguel hesitated. "My mom was sick for a long time. I don't remember when she wasn't sick."

"I'm sorry about your mother, Miguel."

"Let's have a fire in the fireplace tonight, Miguel," said David after the dishes were done. "That's going to be your job. The woodpile is out the back door. You can bring in some tinder and wood. I'll show you how to start the fire."

Miguel sighed but obeyed silently. He returned with an armful of dry wood. David showed him how to lay the tinder and logs. Soon the room was softly lit and warming.

Miguel sat on the floor, poking the embers with a stick. Sparks danced in the rising heat, floating upward.

"Miguel, do you know why you're here?" asked David.

Miguel shook his head. "Not really. My mother

died. I'm alone. The foster lady said I had to move to South Dakota. She said it was where I belonged."

"Your mother was the grandchild of a good man, a Lakota," David explained. "His name was Red Fox. He lived long ago. His best friend, his *kola,* was a boy named Small Bear."

Miguel looked up, recognizing the name.

"Yes, his friend was my grandfather," David said. "They were very close. My grandfather speaks often of his kola Red Fox. They went to boarding school together in Phoenix. When your mother died, the family—*your* family—decided that you needed to be with us. It's a complicated family tree, but you and I are blood. I'm your uncle."

Miguel studied the big man silently.

David continued, "We wanted to see if you would like to live with me. If you don't want to live *here*, there are others in the family who would have you. Family is very important to the Lakota. You have many brothers and sisters. You have many mothers and fathers. You will have a choice."

Miguel nodded. He shoved at the glowing embers again.

"It's okay here, Uncle Small Bear," he said.

4

Kola

The next morning on the bus, a boy hopped on two stops after Miguel. He noticed Miguel and plopped down next to him.

"Hi," he said.

Miguel nodded.

"I'm Nathan," said the boy with a big grin. "Are you the new kid?"

Miguel nodded and hid behind his hair.

"I heard about you. My mom is cousins with a friend of your uncle," Nathan said.

"Oh," said Miguel.

"I think we're in the same class. I skipped school yesterday. I had to take care of my little sister while Dad took Mom to the clinic," continued the chatty Nathan.

"Oh," said Miguel again.

"My mom is sick sometimes. But I don't mind staying home," the boy rattled on.

"Oh," repeated Miguel.

"Guess we'll have to name you Boy Who Talks Much," joked Nathan.

Miguel grimaced. "I'm Miguel."

Nathan grinned. "Glad to meet you, Miguel." Nathan offered Miguel his hand.

Nathan's friendliness chased the butterflies away that morning. In class, Miguel answered the math questions correctly when he had his turn at the board.

But then it was time for Lakota. Miguel hung back, shuffling down the hall behind the rest of the class. Nathan looked back and waited for him.

"Come on, kola. I'll help you," Nathan encouraged.

"*Kola*. That means friend. My uncle told me that," said Miguel.

"See, you catch on fast," said Nathan. He pushed Miguel into the room.

The fawn-eyed teacher smiled at Miguel. Today he caught a word or two. He tried hard to remember the word for buffalo—*tatanka*.

Going home on the bus, Miguel studied the rolling hills of the prairie near the school. They passed freshly turned fields dotted with new green sprout.

"That's my family's winter wheat," explained Nathan. "I got to ride the tractor this year when we tilled and planted. Those are sunflowers on the rise over there. We planted them too. They'll go for seed."

Miguel studied the fields from the bus window. The sunflowers stood upright in the field, row upon row. Past bloom, their blackened faces stared at Miguel. Their heavy heads hung like old men taking a nap after dinner.

The bus slowed. "See ya, kola," called Nathan.

"You said that Bossy would have a calf. When?" asked Miguel. He scratched the buffalo between her horns. Her thick fur tangled in his fingers.

Bossy munched the sage he had offered her. Then she moved off to rub her huge head against a nearby tree. The limbs shook against her weight.

"Next spring. Probably March. Most buffalo have their young in the spring," said David. He pushed back his hat. "Want to give me a hand feeding the horses?" he asked.

"Sure," agreed Miguel. They headed back to the corral next to the barn.

"Can you ride?" asked David. "We could go out to the back range and see the herd, if you like."

"I rode a horse once at the fair," said Miguel. He squared his shoulders and tried to look taller. "I can do it."

"That's a start," David said.

Miguel studied each step as his uncle saddled the spotted horse for him. David gave him a hand up into the saddle.

"It's a long way down," Miguel commented nervously. He felt a few butterflies.

David smiled. "Hold on with your legs and hands. You'll catch on quickly." David swung himself on to his own horse.

"What's the horse's name?" asked Miguel as they headed over the top of the rise.

"Just got her. She used to be named Cissy," said David. "I thought you might want to name her since she's your horse."

"Mine?" squeaked Miguel. Then suspiciously, he added, "You mean mine *today*?"

"No, I mean yours all the time. That is, if you want her. And if you're willing to take care of her," continued his uncle.

They had reached the crest of the hill. Miguel couldn't speak. He had never even had a pet fish. Now he had his own horse. He felt eight feet tall.

Below them spilled another great valley. Endless acres of grass bowed gracefully to the fingers of the wind.

"You have to watch out for prairie dog towns." David pointed to the brown mounds. "Your horse could break a leg in their holes."

"Okay," Miguel agreed.

In the distance, Miguel could see groupings of brown animals. Over the far hilltop, they moved like ants at a picnic.

"Buffalo," Miguel whispered.

"Yes," David said as they stopped to watch the moving herd. "This is close enough today. I want you familiar with your horse before we go out any farther."

Miguel couldn't wait to get home from school the next day. He dashed off the bus and up the hill. He found his uncle repairing the fence near the barn.

"Can I ride today?" asked Miguel breathlessly. "Can I ride my horse? I brought her my apple from lunch. I'm going to name her Phoenix."

David smiled. "Get her saddled up."

Miguel had no trouble catching the filly with an apple as a bribe. However, the saddle was heavy and hard for him to manage. His uncle let him struggle. Finally Miguel noticed the wooden box by the barn. It was just the extra height he needed to hoist the saddle over the patient mare's back.

David showed him how to pick the horse's hooves. Then he gave him a boost into the saddle.

"Have a good ride," he called.

"Aren't you coming?" asked Miguel, suddenly timid.

"Just stay in sight for today," his uncle said. "I have to finish this fence and repair Bossy's too. She keeps trying to break it down."

Miguel still looked worried. David laughed.

"Just remember, *whoa* means stop," David reminded. "And steer clear of any prairie dog towns."

He gave the horse a kindly slap on her haunch. They were off.

Miguel clung to the horn of his saddle for a while. He was terrified that he would find himself on the ground. Soon he caught the rhythm of the horse's easy walk and settled down into the saddle. He checked over his shoulder so as not to lose sight of home.

Miguel was surprised at his thought—home. He looked back at the tiny log cabin in the hollow.

Ahead, at the bottom of the hill, stood the house of their only neighbor. Miguel noticed an old woman hanging clothes on the rickety clothesline. Slowly, he moved closer. Soon he could see her hair, braided in two traditional braids.

Phoenix whinnied. The woman turned and noticed him. She smiled and waved.

Miguel was feeling friendly. He approached, slowing his horse.

"Hello," he called.

"I wondered when you would come for a visit. I have *wasna* if you'd like to stay awhile," she offered.

Her hair was white, and her face was deeply lined with life. Still, she moved quickly toward the door.

"Come," she said as she entered her house.

Miguel struggled to dismount and then remembered to tie his horse. He entered the small home, hesitating awkwardly in the doorway.

A wooden rocker stood next to the fireplace. A small stool rested nearby.

The old woman pointed him toward the stool. She offered Miguel a small pouch with strange brown food in it.

"Wasna," she explained. He took a careful sniff when the old woman looked away. She sat in the creaking rocker. With a wave of her hand, she encouraged him to try it.

Miguel broke off a small bite and cautiously held it to his lips. It smells okay, he thought. It smelled like the strips of meat he could buy at the convenience store in Phoenix.

He took a nibble. It was chewy and rich on his tongue. He decided he liked it.

The old woman nodded as he took another bite.

"What is wasna?" asked Miguel.

"Other Indians call it pemmican. It's what the women made for traveling food. Braves carried it when they went hunting," the old woman explained.

"Does it have berries in it?" asked Miguel, studying the wasna.

"Dried chokecherries," said the old woman.

"Wasna is a very important food for the Lakota," she continued. "It's something we still eat to remember who we are. We are Lakota."

"What's your name?" asked Miguel.

The old woman smiled. "My name is Two Rabbits. But ever since I was a little girl, my family has called me Bunny," she said. "I'm glad you came by, Miguel."

"You know my name?" asked Miguel.

"Yes. The great-grandson of Red Fox has returned.

Soon you will meet all of your family," predicted the woman.

"Are you my family?" asked Miguel.

"No, but there are many who are," she replied.

Miguel studied the small home. Bundles of herbs and dried plants hung from the open rafters. Braided ropes of grass crowded together on a hook on the wall. A painting of a circle of four colors—red, yellow, black, and white—hung above the small fire. The old woman's chair squeaked in quiet companionship.

Miguel heard the crunch of truck wheels on gravel. An engine revved and then died.

"Grandmother Bunny," called a woman's voice.

"There you are," said the woman as she rushed in. "Oh—hello, Miguel."

Miguel stood. He was surprised to see his Lakota teacher standing there.

"Hello," greeted Miguel.

The woman kissed her grandmother. "I brought you the newspaper, Grandmother. And Mother sent some stew for your dinner."

"Thank you," Bunny replied.

"I didn't know you were friends with Miguel," said Miss LaPierre.

"We just now met," stated Bunny.

"I'm sorry I can't stay," Miss LaPierre said. "I must get home and pack for the powwow in Lincoln. I'll be back for you in the morning, Grandmother. Remember, we need to leave by six."

Miss LaPierre hurried back out the door.

"She's always in a hurry," said Bunny, sighing as she sat again. "That's why her Lakota name is Wildfire."

"Does everyone have a Lakota name?" asked Miguel.

"Yes," answered the old woman. "Some of the people use an old family name. Your uncle uses the old name Small Bear as his legal name. He has an English name as well. When we were sent to the mission schools, we were given an English name. Mine was Agatha." She scrunched her nose.

"I never liked that name," she continued. "But most of us have a Lakota name that is given to us because of who we are or what we are like.

"I only have an English name," Miguel said.

"Someday there will be a name that becomes yours. There is time," she assured him.

Miguel savored another mouthful of the wasna.

"Can I take the rest of this with me?" asked Miguel.

"No," replied the old woman, shaking her head. "You must not carry any home. It would be very bad."

She held out her hand and took the remaining wasna from him. "You are in mourning. The ghosts would follow you."

Little chills crept up Miguel's back. Miguel wanted to question her. She held up her hand to stop him and turned toward the fire. Miguel knew it was time to leave.

"Thank you," he whispered as he shut the door.

5

Tunkan (Grandfather)

Miguel studied the ground meat in the small refrigerator. He decided to surprise his uncle and make hamburgers for dinner. Soon he had a meal cooking. He even cleaned and boiled potatoes and cut a loaf of bread.

The table was set when David walked through the door. He looked surprised and then grinned.

"Well," he said. "I guess I do dishes tonight."

The burgers looked delicious, but Miguel crinkled his nose when he tasted his cooking.

David grinned when he noticed Miguel's face. "If you're going to raise buffalo, you'd better get used to eating buffalo," he stated.

Miguel tried to swallow the meat in his mouth. "I can't eat Bossy," he choked.

"It's not Bossy," his uncle assured him. "But we raise buffalo to sell for meat. In the past, Lakota survived on the great herds. We are meat eaters. Buffalo and other game made the people of our tribe strong and healthy.

"It wasn't until we ate the white people's food that we began to sicken. Lakota can't eat too much of this," he said, pointing to the bread. "Many Lakota suffer from the disease diabetes. That is the result of the poor diet we've had to survive on for so many years."

Miguel paled at the mention of the disease. "My mother died of diabetes," he whispered.

"Yes, I know," said David gently. "I hope that raising buffalo to feed our children will help keep the next generation from so much suffering."

Miguel nodded.

"But don't worry," continued his uncle. "We won't

eat Bossy. I could never eat a friend."

After dinner, David did the dishes as promised. Miguel worked on his homework at the kitchen table.

David interrupted Miguel's reading. "Are you ready to meet more of your family?"

Miguel looked up in surprise. He felt a butterfly or two flicker in his stomach. However, curiosity overtook his fear. He shrugged and said, "Sure, when?"

"I thought we might go to my brother's house on Saturday. They live in Wanblee—in Eagle's Nest District. It's a long drive," continued his uncle.

Miguel noticed David's hesitation. "Won't they like me?" he asked.

"Oh, no, Miguel. They can't wait to meet you," insisted David. "I had to beg them to stay away in order to give you some time. I was worried that you're not ready."

Miguel couldn't figure out the warm glow he felt in his chest. He nodded and silently continued reading.

Miguel was quiet on the way to Eagle's Nest. His uncle kept glancing at him but didn't say much.

Finally he pulled the Bronco over and turned to face Miguel. "We don't have to do this."

"It's okay. Really," insisted Miguel. "I just don't

know what to do. What will they want me to do?"

"Just relax and be yourself. They're your family. You don't have to do anything special." David spoke softly.

Miguel nodded.

The village of Wanblee huddled on the prairie. The small cement post office looked like the gathering place. The homes stood in a small cluster off the main highway. They all looked the same, but some showed signs of neglect. A few rusty cars landscaped the yards.

"My brother and his family live here. My sister is down at the end of the street. My parents live next door," his uncle explained as he pulled up to a house. He parked the Bronco.

"How many people are in your family?" asked Miguel.

David smiled. "Well, if you count all your cousins, I think about 45. I have five brothers and three sisters. Most are married and have kids. I'm the youngest."

Miguel paled.

"But don't worry. There are only 15 here today."

Miguel took a deep breath to calm himself. Together, they walked in through the front door. Everyone stopped talking. A withered old man hobbled to face Miguel. Long white hair framed his deep brown face.

David gently placed a hand on Miguel's shoulder.

"Grandfather," he said, "this is Miguel."

The old man put his hands out to Miguel. "Welcome home, *wicatakoza*—grandson."

Miguel didn't try to remember everyone's name. He just accepted the welcoming hugs and friendly smiles. They piled his plate with food and insisted he sit next to Grandfather.

An aunt gave him a knitted hat as a present. Another cousin thrust a beautiful quilt into his arms.

Miguel looked confused and said, "It's not my birthday."

David replied, "Giving gifts is our custom. We're taught to share all we have. These things were made for you."

Grandfather Small Bear's sharp eyes studied Miguel. "You look like him," he finally said.

"Who?" asked Miguel.

"Red Fox, my friend and your great-grandfather," answered Grandfather Small Bear.

"I don't know my family. I only had my mother and now Uncle Small Bear," explained Miguel.

"There's time to know," the old man assured Miguel.

He said something in Lakota to a small child. She left and returned with a leather pouch. It was decorated with a traditional star design. The old man untied the pouch and handed Miguel two small books—one red and one blue.

The old man said, "When my kola returned to Pine Ridge for the last time, he left these with me. I know he would want you to have them."

Miguel opened one of the books. He read the first page. *My name is Red Fox. I am Lakota.*

The old man explained. "When we went to Blackstone Indian School, Red Fox kept a journal. Even after he left school, he continued. I thought it might help you to know him."

"Did he always live at Pine Ridge?" asked Miguel.

"No. Red Fox was born before the reservation. He came home after school but then returned to Phoenix. He married Ellen, a Havasupai girl he met at school. They taught at Blackstone for many years.

"Sometimes he would return to Pine Ridge in the summer, but he loved Blackstone," the old man continued. "He felt he could help so many children there."

"Did you live at Blackstone?" asked Miguel.

"Yes, when I was a boy. It was hard to come back to the reservation. I felt out of place for many years—until I fought in the Great War. Then I understood family," Grandfather Small Bear said. "Your family is your home. And the land . . . the land is what holds us."

Miguel smiled at the old man. "Thank you, sir."

"When you have read them, come and see me again," said Grandfather Small Bear. "I have one more thing to share with you."

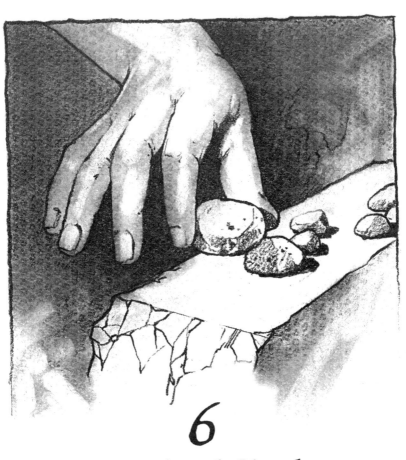

6
Chief Red Cloud

Miguel woke to a loud thump against the house. He had read the journals late into the night. He wanted to know his family.

His bed shook slightly as another whump hit the house.

"Is it an earthquake?" yelled Miguel. He jumped out of bed and slid down the ladder from his loft.

"Buffalo," stated his uncle, still groggy from sleep.

They stood in the doorway, barefoot in the early light. Bossy scratched her head against the corner of the house. She humphed at them good-naturedly.

"She can break down a fence faster than any buffalo," sighed David. "I just fixed it yesterday."

They slipped into coats and shoes. Miguel helped herd Bossy back to her pen. He pulled some sage that grew along the barn wall. He used it to lure her into the pen. David hammered the fallen rail and put up an extra board for good measure.

"Can't blame her," said Miguel's uncle. "She loves the green stuff. Her pasture is getting bare. It's been weeks since it's rained. We'll toss in more hay. Maybe she'll stay put."

"Can't we let her out with the other buffalo?" asked Miguel.

"No, she never does well with the herd," explained David. "She was hand-raised. I think she thinks she's just a big Lakota. If we let her out, the first thing she'd do would be break down the fence to O'Grady's place."

"Who's that?" questioned Miguel. "Nathan mentioned him the other day."

"O'Grady is our neighbor to the north. You couldn't really call him neighborly though. He hates buffalo. He raises some beef cows along with winter wheat. He doesn't think we can get along."

"O'Grady doesn't sound like a Lakota name," said Miguel.

"It's not," his uncle said. "His father bought into the reservation way back. Got a good piece of bottomland. The problem is that O'Grady hates that it's on the reservation. And he hates us."

Miguel didn't understand.

"Don't ever cross the fence to the north," warned David.

"Yes, sir," agreed Miguel, but he was curious.

Fall changed to winter, with days growing shorter. The bright fall leaves of cottonwood and willow covered the dark, damp ground. Work and school routines filled the days. The bus seemed to come earlier every day. It was twilight before home was in sight.

Nathan rode his father's horse to visit Miguel on Sunday afternoon. The boys trotted along the crest of the hill.

"Watch out for the prairie dog town," called Nathan, pointing ahead. "Edge around to the south."

Miguel stopped to watch the furry creatures. They

weren't as active now as they had been in the fall. However, on this warm, still afternoon, a few had ventured up from their snug burrows. Miguel loved to listen to their chirpy warnings and watch the bravest adults hunt for grass.

"It'll snow tonight," said Nathan. He leaned back in the saddle and looked at the heavy gray sky.

"How can you tell?" asked Miguel.

"I can smell it," said Nathan. "That and the weatherman on TV said there was a 90-percent chance."

"Some Indian you are," joked Miguel.

Nathan grinned. "Race ya to O'Grady's fence," he challenged. Nathan gave his filly a quick kick and headed off toward the valley.

Miguel whooped and pushed Phoenix into a gallop. They raced across the open ground. Miguel loved the feel of the cold wind rushing by his cheeks. His eyes stung. His legs and arms tired, but he hung on. He was only two lengths back when they turned at the fence.

"You're getting a lot faster on that horse of yours," complimented Nathan. "I'm going to have to start trying pretty soon."

Miguel tried to look insulted, but he knew he was improving too. "I'll beat you one of these days," he laughed. His horse pranced in excitement.

"What you boys doing here?" a gruff voice called

from behind them. "You know better than to trespass. Or don't you read too well?"

An old man glared at them from under his battered cowboy hat. He was dressed for the cold in a sheepskin coat. A rifle, tucked under one arm, was pointed in their direction.

"We didn't cross the fence," Nathan defended them.

"Who's that?" growled the man. He aimed his rifle in Miguel's direction.

Miguel's mouth went dry.

"This is Miguel, David Small Bear's nephew," explained Nathan. "We aren't trespassing. This is his place."

"Does he speak?" hissed the old man. Miguel studied the man's ice-blue eyes.

"My name is Miguel Torres. My uncle is David Small Bear. I am the great-grandson of Red Fox of the Lakota." Miguel raised his chin. "I am where I belong. Are you?" called Miguel across the prairie.

The old man glared for a moment. He growled something under his breath. Then he silently turned his horse to go. Nathan gave Miguel a thumbs-up. They raced their horses back up the hill. Miguel suddenly felt like shouting.

"I think we could count that as a coup." Nathan grinned as they came to a rest at the top of the hill.

Their horses pranced and blew great breaths of steam into the winter air.

"What's a *coup*?" asked Miguel.

"Long ago, when the Lakota were free, a brave earned coups by doing courageous deeds on the battlefield or the hunt," explained Nathan.

"Like killing the enemy?" asked Miguel.

"Yes, but not just that. It was braver to touch the enemy and then ride away," continued Nathan. "You have held your own with 'One Who Sneers.' That is brave indeed."

"Today we'll go to the grave of Red Cloud, one of our great leaders," explained Miss LaPierre. Miguel's ears perked up. He always enjoyed a field trip.

Outside, the snow was more than a foot deep. It drifted up against the scattered buildings of the school. The sun was out trying to warm the air. It had been weeks of snow and cold.

Miguel was tired of hauling the wood to feed the fireplace, the only heat in the cabin. He was tired of the dark. He was tired of being cold. No one else seemed to be bothered when the thermometer was below zero. Miguel had forgotten what it was like not to shiver. He pulled his hat down so it all but covered his eyes. Then he dug for gloves in his coat pocket.

Miguel was confused when the class didn't head out to the front of the school. Weren't they going to ride the bus? Instead, Miss LaPierre opened a creaky old gate and headed up the hill behind the school.

"How are you doing, Miguel?" she asked. She trudged beside him up the hill.

Miguel smiled. "Fine," he said. "A little cold."

"You'll get used to the cold," laughed Miss LaPierre. "I love the cold of The Tree Popping Moon."

"Tree Popping Moon?" Miguel questioned.

"January," explained Miss LaPierre.

"Why are we going this way?" Miguel asked.

"The grave is just up there," explained Nathan. "Here, have this. You'll need it." Nathan handed Miguel a smooth sandstone pebble.

Now Miguel was really confused.

The class stopped at the top of the bluff. Miguel studied the view of the snow-covered valley and the tiny town of Pine Ridge. The bluff was crowded with old grave markers. Many silvery metal crosses poked their tops above the snow.

Nathan whispered, "The crosses are all the priests and nuns who served at the mission way back in the old days."

The class gathered around a large stone marker. "Most of you know that this is the grave of Chief Red

Cloud. He was a great leader for our people," said Miss LaPierre.

"Red Cloud was a shirtwearer for the Lakota. Shirtwearers were chosen to advise and lead. They devoted their lives to the good of their people. Special shirts were a symbol of their honored position.

"In battle, Red Cloud earned more than 80 coups. He was the only Indian leader who totally defeated the United States in an extended all-out war. Yet he was also a great statesman. He negotiated with presidents so that our people would have a home. When the government wanted to send our children away to boarding schools far from here, he started this school."

The teacher placed a small pebble on the raised stone marker. She said, "He helped our people survive and stay together."

His classmates followed Miss LaPierre's example. Miguel copied the others and placed his pebble.

They crunched through the snow back to the classroom.

"Why did we do that?" Miguel whispered to Nathan.

Nathan dug in his pocket. He showed Miguel three smooth, round stones. One was almost clear quartz. The other two were a deep red color.

"It's a symbol that we are all a part of the world— part of nature. Mother Earth is all around. It is sacred to us," Nathan explained. "Some Lakota carry a few stones with them all the time to remind them of this."

Nathan handed Miguel the clear pebble. Miguel fingered it and then placed it in his pocket.

7

The Black Hills

"Rise and shine," called David. He stood at the base of the ladder to Miguel's loft.

Miguel groaned.

"I want to get an early start," his uncle insisted. "Get up."

"It's Saturday. I don't have to go to school," moaned Miguel.

"Exactly," agreed David. "We're going on a little trip. It's time you saw some of the countryside beyond the reservation."

Miguel was intrigued. He got up and quickly dressed.

"Pack a warm jacket and an extra set of clothes. We'll be gone a few days," continued his uncle.

"Where are we going?" asked Miguel. He hopped down the last three steps.

"Crazy Horse!" said David. There was a gleam in his eye.

Miguel watched as the official reservation sign grew smaller and smaller. They headed across the wide prairie. In the distance, dark, snow-topped mountains rose in the sunrise.

"Those are the Black Hills," explained David. "They are sacred to the Lakota."

"Are they part of the reservation? Do they belong to us?" asked Miguel.

"They should," David said. "They were given to the Sioux Nation as part of the original treaty that the people signed with the U.S. government more than 150 years ago."

"What happened?" asked Miguel.

"Have you ever heard of a man named Custer?" asked David.

Miguel nodded.

"He and some other men found gold in the Black Hills. Even though the government had given that land to the Sioux, they decided they wanted it back."

"But didn't we win when we fought Custer?" asked Miguel.

"We won the battle," agreed his uncle, "but we lost the war. The lands were overrun with settlers and miners. The U.S. government broke its promise."

"Why don't we do something?" exclaimed Miguel. "Couldn't we sue somebody?"

David laughed. "We did. We even won in the Supreme Court. The U.S. government was ordered to give us many millions of dollars."

"Where's the money?" asked Miguel.

"Sitting in the bank," replied David.

"Why?" puzzled Miguel.

"The Black Hills are Mother Earth. We could not sell our mother," insisted David. "Land cannot be sold. We are the land, and it is us."

"But . . ." Miguel struggled to form the question.

"Think of it this way," David said. "Wakan tanka—the Great Mystery—gave us the things we need to live. We take what we need from the land, but it is wrong to take more than you need. For now, we will lend the others the land of the Black Hills. They may use it to feed their children. But we only lend them one foot down. The land will always belong to the Lakota."

Miguel was quiet as he thought about what his uncle had said. Soon they drove past a sign inviting them to the Wind Cave.

"That's a holy place for us," David said. "The spirits speak to the holy men there."

"Can we go there? I'd like to see it," said Miguel hopefully.

"No, we have other things to see today. Someday when it is again a sacred place and not a tourist site, we will go there," said David.

The rolling hills of the plains began to rise and fall. Pine and aspen surrounded them. The spring grass of the prairie waved in the breeze.

They entered Custer State Park. Soon they pulled into a quiet campground.

"Come on," said David. "We can set up camp and then take a hike into the hills."

They set up the tent quickly. Miguel helped David unload the camp gear.

Soon they were following the trail over the high ridge. The air was sweet and still. Miguel felt proud that he could keep up with his uncle's long strides. He knew he had grown three inches since fall.

David stopped and waved Miguel forward. He signaled him to remain silent. He pointed off into the distance.

On the far rise, between two tall pines, stood a

great buffalo. He raised his huge head from grazing in the new green shoots. He stood alone, magnificent against the late afternoon sky. David sat down at the side of the trail. Miguel followed.

David whispered, "Not all the buffalo live in big herds. Often the big males live alone. They're very fierce."

"Do you think he likes it by himself?" asked Miguel.

"It's the life he has chosen," responded his uncle.

The firelight flickered in Miguel's eyes as he studied his uncle. They had grilled buffalo steaks over the fire and made fry bread with honey.

"Let's get to sleep early, Miguel," said his uncle. "We have to be up long before the sun."

"What will we do tomorrow?" asked Miguel.

"Tomorrow we will ride with the buffalo."

It was cold when Miguel awoke. Nearby, the fire glowed with hot embers. Starlight still gleamed overhead. Miguel wanted to stay in the warm bedroll and wait for the sun. He traced the Milky Way across the sky.

David stirred and stretched. He noticed Miguel studying the sky.

"Can you find the Pleides?" David asked.

Miguel shook his head. "But Nathan showed me where Orion is—and the belt," he answered. He pointed to three bright stars in a row.

"Look over to the center," his uncle instructed. "There are seven stars very close together in the Pleides. There are also seven tribes in the Sioux Nation."

"I could never see the stars in Phoenix. Here they seem so close," commented Miguel dreamily.

"Too much city," said David. He rose to stir the fire and begin the day.

Before the dawn streaked the sky, Miguel and his uncle were at the main corral. Borrowed horses, saddled and ready, waited patiently at the fence.

"These horses have worked the buffalo before— just as ours at home have," said David. He cinched the leather strap tighter under the horse's belly.

"Miguel, you must stay close to me unless I tell you otherwise. Don't get in front of the herd. It's a small herd, but they could trample you just the same."

"Why are we doing the roundup now?" asked Miguel. "I thought they did this in the fall."

"The rangers need to round up the buffalo herd in the park and check them for disease. There's been some brucellas in nearby cattle ranches," explained David. "Even though the herd has been vaccinated against it, the ranchers are concerned the disease came from the buffalo. We must prove that it didn't."

With two dozen other riders, they trotted off across the prairie. A few battered pickup trucks lumbered along behind.

Stopping at a rise on the hill, Miguel could view the sunrise in the east. It cast long golden shadows on the rolling landscape.

Pine and aspen crowded the crests of the hills. Snow still hid in northern notches. The grass was newly green with spring warmth. It sported small splashes of prairie flowers—yellow, orange, and purple.

In a hollow, the buffalo grazed. Their breath steamed in the morning cold.

"We need to drive them through that gap and along the river bottom," explained David. "The corrals are a few miles from here." He pointed toward the sunrise. "If we move in now while the buffalo are quiet, they won't scatter."

David signaled for the trucks to stay back. "The horses are quieter," he explained.

The horsemen surrounded the herd on three sides like a big horseshoe. They eased forward quietly, step by step. David signaled a rider to move forward on the far side, blocking an escape route.

"If we get the lead buffalo started in the right direction," explained his uncle quietly, "then the others will follow. It's just a matter of keeping them together."

The buffalo had noticed the riders by now. The lookout animals snorted their warning. Others who had been resting rose and humphed. They were irritated.

A mother and her new calf made a desperate run for the trees. Two riders chased them down and turned them back to the main herd. Slowly, the riders moved forward. Whistling and shouting, they guided the herd along.

One rider held a long whip. He cracked it in the air. The sharp echo filled the small canyon. The last lazy buffalo moved along.

"Stay to the outside," called his uncle. The herd picked up speed.

Miguel nodded. They increased their speed to a quick trot. Suddenly the herd swerved in his direction. Miguel found himself riding in a stream of huge woolly animals. He felt the surge of movement, rushing with them like a great brown river.

His uncle signaled him to move back. He was concerned for Miguel's safety.

But Miguel felt no fear. He could almost feel the bow in his hand. He understood what it must have been like to live free, depending on this great animal for his needs—his life. Somehow, he knew what his ancestors knew.

Suddenly he saw a break in the herd. Miguel moved from harm's way back to his uncle's side. He was grinning as he approached.

"Too close!" shouted David.

They rushed down the valley, across the small creek running with icy snow melt. The buffalo moved as one, flowing across the hillside like a splash of mercury. Thunder filled the air from thousands of galloping hooves on the rocky earth. They funneled into a narrow gulch, crowding together. The buffalo were huffing and angry now.

The riders pushed the herd forward, shouting and calling. The whip cracked through the air like lightning. Dust rose in great clouds.

"Don't let them turn!" shouted his uncle.

Miguel waved his hat and hollered. He edged some wayward yearlings back into the group. The lead buffalo squeezed through the wide gate ahead.

"Keep them moving!" David yelled. A few stubborn mothers slipped through the riders. Their calves struggled to keep up. Soon they were recaptured and flowed back into the brown river.

The riders gave a last whoop as the gates were closed on the herd. Inside, the annoyed buffalo circled and humphed. Soon they found the piles of hay that were set out to soothe them.

"Cool!" was all Miguel could think to say.

David joined him near the gate. He smiled at the look on Miguel's face.

"That has got to be the best thing I've ever done," stated Miguel. They were breaking up camp and loading up the Bronco. "Can I help when *we* have a roundup? Can I learn to rope the calves? Wait until I tell Nathan at school!"

David smiled.

"Where are we going now?" asked Miguel. The truck had left Custer State Park behind. They were headed north, traveling through pine-dotted hills and high prairie.

"Look over at the mountain," suggested David.

Miguel squinted into the distance. A high rocky peak rose above them.

"There's a face!" exclaimed Miguel. "I can see a horse's head."

They stopped before the entrance to study the view.

"Crazy Horse," David said.

On the mountainside, Miguel saw a quick flash. Gray rock exploded into the air. Another flash followed. Finally the echoing booms reached them.

"They're working on the monument today," his uncle explained.

As they entered the museum, a guard encouraged them to sit and watch a movie about the Crazy Horse Monument.

"In a minute," said Miguel's uncle. "Let's go see if they're going to set off some more explosives."

Miguel dashed to the edge of the deck. He wiggled through the crowd to get a front view.

"Can you see the men up there?" David asked. "They're standing along the ridge that will be Crazy Horse's arm."

Miguel squinted and nodded.

"There should be some more charges soon," David predicted.

Miguel studied the huge mountain. He imagined the Lakota horseman running into the wind, his hair flying. Man and rider seemed to be pushing— struggling to escape from their rock imprisonment.

A loud whistle shrilled. The men working on the mountain had disappeared. The crowd hushed.

Boom! More explosions traced along the front of the horse's face. Rock spewed into the air. The blast echoed off the canyons, bouncing back again and again. The crowd cheered and clapped.

"No more today, folks," called the official.

"We read about Crazy Horse in Lakota class. He

was a great warrior. He outsmarted everyone and won many battles against the cavalry. He never gave up," Miguel informed his uncle.

"I came here when I was your age," said David. "My grandfather brought me. Then it was only old Ziolkowski on the hill. He worked by himself most of the time in the early years. There was just a trailer then, not a big museum. You could only just make out where Crazy Horse's nose was going to be. It's taken a lifetime to get it this far."

"Is it as big as Rushmore, where the presidents are?" asked Miguel. "I saw a picture of that in my history book."

"Bigger," replied David. "Much bigger. When it's done, it will be the largest statue in the world."

"Hello, Miguel," said a quiet, familiar voice. "I didn't know you'd be here."

Miguel turned in surprise to see his Lakota teacher.

"My uncle brought me." Miguel introduced the two adults.

David took Miss LaPierre's hand and smiled at her. She smiled back shyly.

"I try to come every time they're doing a set of explosions. Somehow it's so exciting to watch Crazy Horse be freed," she said. "It's nice to see you, David. My grandmother told me you're ranching near her."

"Yes. When did you come back from the

university?" David asked.

"Just this fall," she said. "I'm teaching at Red Cloud."

Miguel studied the two adults in a moment of awkward silence.

"Well . . . I'd better go now," said Miss LaPierre finally.

Miguel and David wandered through the museum. David let Miguel stop and study anything that was interesting to him.

"She's pretty," commented Miguel.

"Hmm? Oh, you mean your teacher?" his uncle asked. He pretended to look the other way. "Yes, she was always very pretty."

"So you knew her before?" pestered Miguel.

"Uh, yes," David admitted.

"She's not married, is she?" asked Miguel. David shook his head.

Exasperated, Miguel said, "Well . . ."

"Well what?" questioned his uncle.

"Ask her out. She's over there. Go on," urged Miguel. "I'll stay right here."

His uncle looked embarrassed.

"I could do it if you're too shy," offered Miguel.

"No. I've been meaning to go see her all winter," said David. He headed back to speak to Miss LaPierre.

Miguel tried not to be too obvious as he peeked

over his shoulder to watch his uncle. He couldn't hear their words. The look on his uncle's face told him the good news.

"We're going riding next weekend," he filled Miguel in. Miguel gave him a high five. They went off to get ice cream.

8
Buffalo Calf

It was late when David and Miguel returned to the cabin. Without a moon, the night was dark. A light spring frost touched the new grass. Miguel struggled to wake up enough to climb the ladder to his loft.

David called, "I'll see you in the morning. I'm going to check on Bossy before I turn in." He closed the door behind him.

Miguel dumped his shoes on the floor. He was too tired to change into his pajamas. He collapsed on the bed with a satisfied smile. He closed his eyes and waited for his uncle to return from the barn and turn off the light below.

He must have dozed a few minutes. Then he woke with a start. Somehow he knew he was still alone in the house. He rose and checked the clock on the shelf. More than an hour had passed.

Miguel stuffed his feet back into his shoes. He grabbed his coat. It hung on its hook by the door. He opened the door, feeling the cold air. As his eyes adjusted, the Milky Way lit the way. He headed for the dim outline of the barn. A light burned inside. It escaped through the cracks in the old door.

Miguel opened the creaky, worn wood. "Uncle Small Bear?"

Miguel heard rustling and a low grunt. The hairs on Miguel's arms stood on end.

"Over here," said David in a low voice.

Miguel entered the stall. It was covered with fresh hay. Bossy lay on the floor. David knelt at the great animal's head, stroking her shaggy mane. Her eyes were glazed in pain, white at the edge. She humphed again, pawing the air with her front legs.

"What's wrong?" asked Miguel in a panic.

"Nothing," replied his uncle. "She was in labor

when I came to check on her." David saw the worried look on Miguel's face.

"Is she going to die?" asked Miguel.

"Everything is going just fine, Miguel. I could use your help though. Come and sit here. Stroke her and talk to her. She knows you. I want to check the position of the calf."

Miguel swallowed the lump sticking in his throat. He sat in the fragrant hay.

"It's okay, Bossy," he cooed at her. "You're going to be a mama soon. I bet you can't wait to see your new baby."

Bossy arched against him. Miguel felt her straining against the pain. Tears sprung to his eyes.

"She's hurting!" he cried to his uncle.

"Almost there, Miguel. Keep her down," David ordered.

Bossy made a strange moaning sound. Miguel was afraid to take his eyes off the big animal's face.

"Look, Miguel!" David said, suddenly very excited.

David rubbed a small, wet creature with clean rags and fresh hay. It bleated and struggled to right itself. It called to Bossy. The mother buffalo responded with a deep, satisfied grunt.

"Wow," said Miguel.

All legs, the calf finally found its four feet. It stood, wobbling.

"Come and rub her down some more," ordered his uncle softly.

Miguel took the rag and brushed the baby's face. Its raspy tongue kissed Miguel's hand. He laughed and hugged the baby. It smelled brand-new.

Bossy returned to her feet.

"Let her nurse," said David. The baby nudged her mother's belly, finding her first rich meal.

David and Miguel studied Bossy and her new calf from the far side of the stall.

"Good job, Miguel," congratulated David.

Miguel was surprised when he opened the barn door. It was light outside. The last pink of sunrise was fading slowly.

"It's the tradition of our people that a new creature or person's name is something that is seen soon after its birth," said David. "Miguel, you should name the calf."

Miguel thought for just a moment.

"Her name is Sunrise."

9

Powwow

Miguel and Nathan hung over the pasture fence. They were watching Sunrise prance in the new green grass. The fast-growing calf bleated happily to Bossy. Bossy responded with a patient "humph."

The boys had to laugh as the little buffalo barreled across the pasture and slammed into her mother. She was looking for a quick snack.

"She's a nice calf," said Nathan. "That's cool that you got to help. I help my dad when the horses foal."

Miguel nodded.

"Why aren't they out with the rest of the herd?" asked Nathan. "Buffalo usually don't need to be penned."

Miguel explained. "I guess Bossy was raised away from the herd. We're her family. Uncle Small Bear is going to try to put her and her calf back into the herd soon. Then Sunrise will know how to be a buffalo."

A little disappointed, he continued, "I'm not supposed to pet her too much. That way she won't think she's a person. My uncle calls it bonding."

"I know what you mean," said Nathan. "I had this little chick once that I raised. It would follow me around everywhere. What a pest! It thought I was its mama."

Miguel climbed up and stood on the lower fence rail. He studied the gathering gray clouds to the north. A rumble of thunder rolled down the valley.

"Better get in the house," suggested Nathan. A flash of lightning crackled across the prairie. The storm hung in the humid air. Rain grayed the land below, drenching it.

Miguel and Nathan met David at the front door of the house. The wind gusted around them. The thunder, now deafening, filled the air.

"Get inside, boys," called Miguel's uncle.

"What about Bossy and Sunrise?" yelled Miguel above the howl of the wind.

"They're fine," he said, closing the door against the wind. "Buffalo are built for the prairie. They just lower down and wait it out. Their coats keep them warm and dry."

"My dad says that buffalo put their face first into the wind even in a blizzard," agreed Nathan. "They survive a lot better than cattle."

Still a little worried, Miguel watched out the window. The brief fury of the storm traveled down the valley. He couldn't even see the white rock battlements across the way. Hail bounced off the roof of the cabin.

Then, just as quickly, it was over. The hail stopped. The thunder dimmed. The lightning ceased.

Miguel dashed out the door and down to the pasture. Bossy lay curled in the glistening grass. Knees under her, she quietly chewed her cud. Sunrise's coat sparkled with raindrops. She nipped a leaf of white sage as she flicked her long tail.

Miguel sighed quietly in relief.

"I have to get home soon," said Nathan. "My mom is taking me to Rapid City for the weekend to dance at the powwow."

"Is that fun?" asked Miguel. "I've never been to a powwow."

"Really?" exclaimed Nathan.

Miguel shrugged.

"They're fun," Nathan said. "I have a new costume that my mom and grandmother sewed for me. It's blue with long fringe. It has a real eagle-feather bustle.

"In the big powwows, you can even earn money for dancing. My sister is a hoop dancer. She's really good and earns money that way. She's saving to go to college.

"But I really like the ones on the reservation best. Then you know everyone. It's like a big party."

Nathan's face lit up with an idea.

"Do you think your uncle would let you go with us? There's room in the camper, and we'll be back tomorrow. Let's go ask him."

Miguel hesitated.

Nathan pushed Miguel. "Go ask, kola. It'll be fun."

In the barn, David was throwing down hay from the loft onto the floor below.

"Can . . ." began Miguel.

Before he could finish, David smiled and said, "Yes, go get packed. Don't forget a coat."

Miguel let out a whoop. He dashed back to the house.

Nathan climbed on to his horse bareback.

"We'll be back to pick you up in an hour," he called. He waved as he galloped off.

Miguel bit into his second piece of fry bread. The honey dripped down his chin. "Mmm" was all his mouth could say.

Nathan just nodded.

"Hurry, Miguel. I still have to finish getting dressed. My dance is at 8:00."

The boys wandered back through the vendors' booths. They studied crafts and artwork.

Nathan's family had pitched a tent roof in the large circle surrounding the arena. Under the tent, Nathan finished putting on his costume. He pulled on a spiky headdress.

"You look like a punk rocker," teased Miguel.

Nathan grinned and nodded his head. The decoration on his head swayed.

"It's porcupine fur," he stated, pointing to his hat. "My mom just finished it last night. She's been working on the beadwork all winter."

Tiny glistening beads sparkled across Nathan's shoulders and down his sleeves. His soft kid moccasins were decorated in the same star pattern of red and blue.

Long fringe swayed from his arms and legs. Nathan's grandmother attached the eagle-feather bustle at his waist. Nathan took up his decorated shield.

The announcer called for Nathan and four other boys to step into the center of the arena. Miguel studied the other boys, all in beaded costumes of bright colors.

To the side of the arena, four men sat in a circle around a huge skin drum. In unison, they began to beat the great drum. The elder began the song, with the other men chiming in. A hypnotic pulse filled the air.

Nathan let the song fill him. He began to move to the music. The elder called the words of the song, wailing at times. Miguel could understand only a few of the words. But he could feel the music within.

He watched Nathan twirl and bend. He kicked and lunged to the song. The boys weaved slowly in a circle. Their feet tapped lightly on the soft ground. Miguel wished . . .

Then the music stopped for just a moment. The dancers waited. They started up for one more measure. Then silence. Grinning, Nathan walked off the arena as spectators clapped.

Miguel smiled and said, "That was great, kola."

"The next dance everyone can join. Do you want to try?" said Nathan.

Miguel looked unsure.

"I'll show you. You can even borrow my other

costume," urged his friend.

"Okay," said Miguel with a shrug.

"Great," said Nathan. He ran to get Miguel the costume. Miguel struggled into a green shirt with short fringe.

"Could I carry your shield?" he asked Nathan hesitantly.

"Sure. This is a blanket dance. Here's a dollar. The money goes to help the veterans. Just do what I do," continued Nathan.

The boys walked into the arena and put their money on the blanket. Then they approached the older men at the head of the dance group. Some were dressed in parts of a military uniform.

Nathan solemnly shook each man's hand. Miguel followed. He remembered to lower his eyes to show respect for his elders.

Then the boys fell in line with all the people. The drumbeat filled the air. Miguel watched Nathan's feet for a few minutes until he knew what to do. He copied the simple bouncing step.

"It's easy," said Miguel, catching on quickly.

They followed the veterans around the wide arena. Other people—some native, some not—joined in until the blanket filled with contributions.

Nathan gave a quick kick in the air and lunged forward.

"Try it," he urged Miguel.

Miguel's kick wasn't so high, but he kept to the music. He heard the elders sing the old song. Although many people watched the dance from the sidelines, Miguel danced for himself and for Red Fox.

10
Showdown

Across the valley, a fat orange moon crept over the top of the battlements. Miguel waited on the front steps as Nathan hurried up the drive. He waved when he noticed Miguel.

"Thanks for coming," said Miguel.

Nathan grinned. "Now I don't have to baby-sit my little sister. Did your uncle already leave?" he asked.

Miguel nodded. "He went to pick up Miss LaPierre. The concert at the community center starts soon."

"Hot date," kidded Nathan, with a little jab to Miguel's ribs.

Miguel grinned. "He was a nervous wreck. I think he really likes her a lot."

"Cool," said Nathan.

"We have to wait until it's really dark," said Nathan as he studied the night sky. "Let's go see what there is to eat."

"Really dark for what?" asked Miguel, following him into the cabin.

Nathan smiled mysteriously.

After popcorn and gin rummy, Nathan finally explained.

"Have I ever told you about tipping cows?" he asked.

Miguel had heard about the prank at school. He ignored a twinge of conscience and smiled.

"It's the perfect night," said Nathan.

"Won't we get caught?" worried Miguel.

"No. Come on. It doesn't hurt anyone," urged Nathan. "I've done it lots of times. My cousins showed me how."

"Okay," agreed Miguel.

"Put on your dark jacket and a hat," instructed Nathan.

Miguel followed his friend out the door and across the fields. Miguel hesitated at the fence to O'Grady's land.

"I don't know . . ." whispered Miguel. "My uncle told me to stay away."

"No one will ever know," whispered Nathan.

He held the barbed wire for Miguel to crawl under. Soon they had crossed the old man's pasture. They lay on their stomachs at the rise of a hill studying the field below. A dozen cattle stood quietly. The house in the distance was dark.

Miguel's heart raced in his chest. "Are you sure we won't get caught?" he hissed to Nathan.

"We'll be fine. I'll show you how. Just stay low and quiet," said Nathan.

Nathan quietly trotted toward the nearest cow. As he came close, he slowed. He carefully sneaked up on the sleeping animal. Then, with a mighty heave, he shoved the cow. It tipped over with a thud onto the soft ground. Its legs stuck straight out as it continued to snooze. Nathan was giggling as he rejoined Miguel on the hill.

"It didn't wake up," laughed Miguel. "It's still sound asleep. Will it be okay?"

"Doesn't hurt a bit," Nathan assured him. "It will just sleep there the rest of the night." The two boys snickered. "Now *you* try," encouraged Nathan.

Miguel swallowed his fear. He raced across the open pasture to the nearest sleeping cow. Quietly, he tiptoed to its side. He could hear the quiet breathing as he placed his hands on the cow's side. He shoved with all his might, but the cow didn't budge.

Nathan started across the pasture to help. Suddenly, O'Grady's dogs began to bark. A light went on in the cabin.

Nathan stopped and then let out a warning whistle. Miguel couldn't breathe. He couldn't move.

Nathan hissed, "Kola, come on. O'Grady will be here in a minute."

They raced across the open pasture. O'Grady was out the door and yelling at them. His dogs barked and began to chase the boys. Miguel felt as if his feet were made of lead. He gasped for air.

The dogs were howling as they dashed across the pasture. O'Grady hurled angry curses at the boys. They dove under the barbed wire and wiggled through. Miguel caught the sleeve of his jacket.

"I'll get you devils!" yelled the angry old man.

The boys raced up the drive and slammed the door of the cabin behind them.

"Will he come get us?" whispered Miguel, trying

to catch his breath. He wiped the cold sweat from his brow.

Nathan peered out the corner of the window. "I don't see him. I think he stopped at the fence."

They waited in silence, listening to the far-off barking of the dogs. Miguel could feel his heart still pounding.

Nathan turned to Miguel. He slapped him on the shoulder.

"I told you it was fun," he said with a grin.

Spring vacation finally came. Miguel got off the bus with a hoot. He ran all the way up the dusty road. He flung his backpack into the cabin and dashed down to the pasture.

Phoenix neighed as he whistled to her. She trotted over and waited while Miguel gently placed the bit in her mouth. Miguel liked riding bareback. He gave the filly a light tap in the ribs and trotted her through the open gate.

Nathan was approaching on his horse. Miguel waved.

"Which way do you want to ride?" asked Nathan as he pulled up beside Miguel.

Miguel answered, "Let's go out to check the herd

for Uncle Small Bear first. Then we can go on over to the creek."

"Great," agreed Nathan.

The boys walked their mounts around the prairie dog town. The little creatures chirped a warning and then skittered for cover as they approached.

Then the boys raced across the open prairie to the buffalo. Miguel knew the herd would be down by the creek. They'd be resting in the shade of the willows on this warm afternoon.

He urged Phoenix forward into a gallop. He couldn't wait to see how Sunrise was adjusting to the herd. It had been a whole week since they had let Bossy and Sunrise back out on the range. David had told the boys not to visit the herd or disturb Bossy. They needed time with other buffalo. Miguel had promised just to observe from the hilltop above the creek.

The boys laughed as they jumped a small rivulet. A spray of droplets splashed into the air. They stopped at the hilltop and scanned the buffalo below.

"We're downwind," said Miguel. "They shouldn't notice that we're here."

"Do you see Sunrise?" asked Nathan.

Miguel searched among the new mothers and their calves. Bossy was bigger than most of the females. She was usually easy to find, even in the large herd. Miguel had learned to distinguish many members of the herd. He secretly named them. There was Old Baldy, the bull with a white patch on his head. There was Shaggy and Scooby-Doo . . .

A loud rifle crack split the quiet afternoon. Nathan looked as surprised as Miguel did.

"It came from O'Grady's place," Nathan said, pointing north.

Miguel's heart stopped as he noticed the trampled fencing that unsuccessfully divided his uncle's property from "One Who Sneers." He searched the herd once again for Bossy.

"Oh, no," Miguel whispered to himself. His stomach lurched into his throat. "Not Bossy."

Miguel gave his horse a hard kick and pointed her toward the broken fence. They tore across the range. Nathan yelled and then followed. Miguel rode onto O'Grady's land.

Nathan shouted, "Miguel, wait!"

Nathan hesitated at the fence. Miguel didn't listen.

Nathan cried, "He'll kill you if you trespass!"

Miguel turned Phoenix. "It's Bossy," he choked. "She's not in the herd."

Nathan understood. "Come on," he said. He gave his horse a swift kick.

The boys rode over the crest of the next hill. They spotted O'Grady on horseback below them. He had his rifle pointed at Sunrise, who hovered near her dying mother.

"No!" yelled Miguel. He raced past O'Grady. The old man took aim. Miguel jumped from his horse and stood in front of the buffalo calf. "No!"

"She's trespassing," growled the old man. "And so are you."

Nathan caught up. He slapped the old man's horse hard with his hand. The horse reared in surprise. O'Grady fell with a thump to the ground. The rifle fired harmlessly into the air. Nathan jumped down and kicked the gun away.

Miguel held on to the calf. For the first time, he looked down at Bossy. She lay crumpled beside him, struggling to catch her breath.

Too much blood was all Miguel could think. The beautiful buffalo looked him solemnly in the eye. Then she sighed and was gone.

The old man slowly picked himself up off the ground. He dusted off his worn cowboy hat and placed it on his head.

"Don't you touch her!" shouted Miguel. "Don't you touch Bossy or her baby."

For a moment, Miguel thought O'Grady might get the gun and shoot them all. Then the old man turned and slowly walked away.

Miguel, his arms still around the calf, sank to his knees and sobbed.

Nathan touched Miguel's shoulder. "I'll go get

help," he said softly.

Miguel wouldn't leave Bossy until Nathan returned with David. Grandmother Bunny and Miss LaPierre came too.

"He just murdered Bossy!" cried Miguel. "He didn't have to do that. She wasn't hurting anything. It's all my fault."

His uncle held Miguel as the sobs crashed through him. Nathan put a halter on Sunrise and slowly led her home. She bleated, afraid to leave her mother's side.

Grandmother Bunny took an abalone shell from the pouch she was carrying. She lit a braid of sweet grass, letting the smoldering embers fall into the shell. A fragrant smoke lingered as she added white sage to the flame. She chanted in a low voice, moving the shell over the buffalo.

"Would you like to say good-bye?" asked David. Miguel could hear the choke in his uncle's voice.

Miguel brushed the tears from his eyes and asked, "What is Grandmother Bunny doing?"

"She is blessing tatanka. She is giving the spirit of our friend release from this life," explained Miss LaPierre.

Grandmother Bunny continued with the quiet prayer. Miguel reached out and brushed Bossy's long mane. His fingers tangled in her soft fur.

Then they all turned for home.

Nathan locked Sunrise in the barn stall. The buffalo calf bawled anxiously for her mother. Miguel and the grown-ups joined Nathan. They studied the little calf.

"There's not much we can do," sighed David.

Miss LaPierre said sadly, "Maybe if she were a little older."

"What do you mean?" asked Miguel.

Miss LaPierre explained, "She's an orphan, Miguel. She's too young to be without her mother."

"We could get one of the other new mothers to take her," insisted Miguel.

"It would never work," his uncle said. "We can't let her starve. It's the only thing to do."

Miguel's eyes got wide with horror as he realized what his uncle was saying.

"No!" he shouted. "No. You can't."

David looked stricken.

"*I* could raise her," suggested Miguel. "Nathan could help me."

David shook his head.

"Why not?" argued Miguel. "*You* raised Bossy."

"Bossy wasn't this young," David replied. "And it almost didn't work even then. She would suffer, Miguel. You can't let an animal suffer."

David turned to leave the barn. Miguel knew the

rifle was locked away in the cabin. He had to think quickly.

"Give me a few days," Miguel pleaded. "If she isn't thriving, I'll do it myself. Please let me try. This is my fault. I have to try."

David sighed and turned back to Miguel. He rubbed his face with his hand, frustrated.

"Three days, no more, Miguel," he agreed finally. "She has to be eating fully by then. Otherwise it's no good."

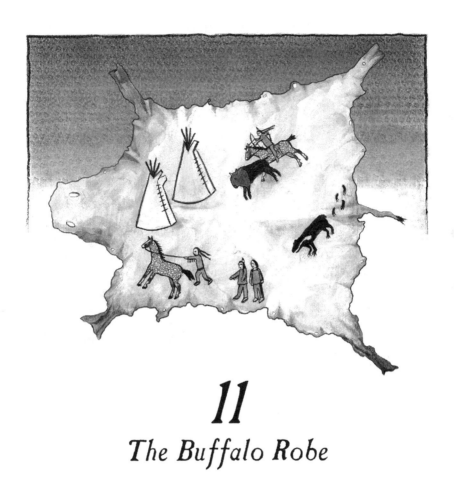

11
The Buffalo Robe

Miguel ached with fatigue and frustration. He had spent the evening trying to convince Sunrise that the bottle of formula was good for her. The buffalo calf chewed halfheartedly on the oversized nipple. Miguel tried squeezing a bit of the milk into her mouth. He ended up with both of them dripping.

Sunrise bawled and listened for her mother's return call. Finally she curled up in the corner, miserable. Miguel covered her with a blanket and nestled down next to her.

"Tomorrow, Sunrise. Tomorrow will be a better day. I promise," whispered Miguel.

Sunrise's ears twitched. She closed her eyes to rest.

"How is she doing?" asked Nathan from the other side of the wall. Miguel stretched and rubbed his eyes. Dawn light streamed through the door.

"Lousy," he whispered. "But at least she's stopped moaning."

"That's not good," said Grandmother Bunny, entering the barn behind Nathan.

Miss LaPierre followed them in.

"She was up three times in the night, but she won't drink from the bottle," sighed Miguel.

"We have an idea," said Miss LaPierre. She held a large brown skin.

"Buffalo calves know their mamas by sound and smell," explained Grandmother Bunny.

"So we brought Sunrise her mama's smell," Nathan continued.

Miguel stared at the buffalo hide in growing horror. "Bossy?" he whispered.

The old woman studied Miguel's horrified face.

She patted him, saying, "Nothing from tatanka should ever be wasted. That has always been our way. If this can save your little Sunrise, is that not better that letting it rot on the prairie?"

"I found Grandmother Bunny stretching the hide this morning," explained Nathan. "It gave me the idea. Come on, Miguel. Put the robe over you, and hold the bottle for Sunrise."

Miguel shrugged. "It might just work."

He carried the heavy robe to the baby and wrapped himself with it. The smell of the fresh skin gave him the willies. He nestled next to Sunrise and humphed. Then he placed the nipple near her mouth.

Sunrise let out a welcoming bawl. Fiercely, she grabbed the nipple and sucked. She drained the bottle in a few minutes.

"It's working," called Miguel. "Get another bottle."

After most of the second bottle was gone, Sunrise settled in the new hay with a full stomach.

The next two days were a blur for Miguel. He fed Sunrise every three hours, day and night. Nathan volunteered to take the second night, but Miguel refused to leave the barn. So Miguel slept in a blanket in the corner while Nathan fed the calf.

In the early morning light of the third day, Nathan balanced the bottle for Sunrise. He rested his head on the stable wall. His eyes were drooping with sleep. He fought to stay awake against the glugging noise of the baby buffalo's breakfast.

Miguel stretched and opened his eyes. "Long night?" he asked his friend.

Nathan nodded with a low groan.

"I'll take over," offered Miguel.

"That's okay. She's almost done. She should sleep for a bit now," said Nathan with a big yawn.

Miguel noticed the light seeping in the crack of the barn door. "It's just getting light."

"Did you finish that book?" asked Nathan. He glanced toward one of Red Fox's journals. It was sitting on a wooden box next to Miguel.

Miguel nodded.

"Red Fox was . . . amazing," he said as he picked up his great-grandfather's journal. "He had to leave everything he knew behind when he went to Blackstone."

"He was an orphan too, wasn't he?" asked Nathan.

"Yeah." Miguel took a quick breath. "Red Fox learned about his father and mother from a buffalo robe that his mother painted. I saw a robe in the museum at Crazy Horse, but it was different."

"I heard about Red Fox's robe," said Nathan.

"There was a buffalo hunt painted on it," said

Miguel. "And a picture of his father's horse. The robe told stories about his father and the Lakota ways before things changed."

Miguel paused for a moment, lost in thought.

"The journal doesn't say what happened to the robe," he said finally. "I bet it got lost.

"It would have been so cool to see it," he added.

Miguel picked up the journal and went to face the rising sun.

David brought the morning bottles in. "Good thing it's spring break."

Miguel smiled as he offered the bottle to the hungry calf.

"She's figured out that she doesn't need the robe," explained Miguel. Soft glugging noises continued until the bottle was drained.

"I think we'll need bigger bottles soon," said David.

Sunday afternoon was warm and sunny. The boys led Sunrise into the pasture. She followed Miguel, never straying far from him.

"What do I do now?" he asked. "She won't let me out of her sight."

David smiled.

Miss LaPierre said, "Tough being a parent, isn't it? You've done a good job, Miguel. She has grown this week."

Miguel rubbed the baby's soft, curly face. Sunrise nuzzled close.

"It's time for her to grow up just a little," said David. "Go up and take a quick shower. We'll stay with her."

Miguel looked doubtful but climbed over the fence. The baby bawled as Miguel made his way to the cabin.

"I'll be back, Sunrise," he called.

Miguel watched as Sunrise nibbled on new green clover. He turned when he heard the Bronco rumble up the road. Miguel was surprised to see Grandfather Small Bear riding next to his uncle.

Miguel ran and helped the old man slowly make his way to the cabin.

"It's good to see you, Grandfather," said Miguel. "Did you hear about my buffalo calf?"

"Yes." Small Bear nodded. "That was clever to trick the calf."

"That was Nathan's idea. He's my kola," said Miguel.

After the old man sat, Miguel settled on the floor

by the fireplace. "I've read my great-grandfather's journals," he said.

"Good," said the old man. "I've brought you the other thing I promised to share with you."

Miguel's uncle unwrapped the large parcel he had carried in from the truck.

"What is it?" asked Miguel.

Miguel peered into the package. He caught his breath.

"It's the buffalo robe! It's Red Fox's robe. You have it!" exclaimed Miguel.

"I have brought it to you," the old man said.

"I wondered what happened to it after Red Fox gave it to his friend Fern," said Miguel.

"Years later, after Fern had married her husband Paul, she saw Red Fox again. She had kept her promise to protect the robe," explained Grandfather Small Bear.

Miguel unwrapped the robe and studied the paintings.

"That's Brave Colt," he whispered. "And Clover."

"Yes," said Grandfather Small Bear. "These are your people. I think the robe should be yours."

Miguel could almost feel the gentle wind blow through his hair. He knew the fragrance of the sweet grass and sage of the prairie.

Miguel turned to his uncle. "It is our way to be given a name—a Lakota name."

His uncle nodded.

"I am Red Fox," said Miguel. He stood proudly. "I am Lakota."